Twenty Clay Children

Written by Elizabeth Lane

Illustrated by Brenden Taylor

Here are 20 clay children.
They want to hear a story.

"Come," calls the storyteller.
"Sit and listen."

20 clay children try to climb
onto the storyteller's lap.

There is no room. So they climb on
her arms, legs, and head.

"Oh!" cries the storyteller.
"This will not work!"

"20 children won't fit."

The potter comes over.

She makes a new clay shape.

20 clay children watch.
What will it be?

The potter bakes the clay,
lets it cool, and paints it.

20 children cheer!
It is another storyteller!

10 clay children on each lap.

20 happy clay children!